Instructions for using AR

LET AUGMENTED REALITY CHANGE HOW YOU READ A BOOK

With your smartphone, iPad or tablet you can use the **Hasmark AR** app to invoke the augmented reality experience to literally read outside the book.

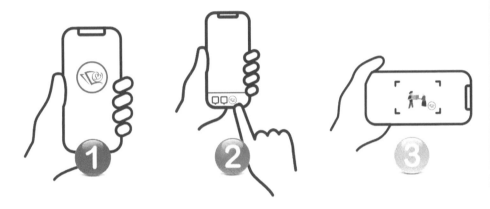

1. Download the **Hasmark app** from the **Apple App Store** or **Google Play**

2. Open and select the (vue) option

3. Point your lens at the full image with the and enjoy the augmented reality experience.

Go ahead and try it right now with the Hasmark Publishing International logo.

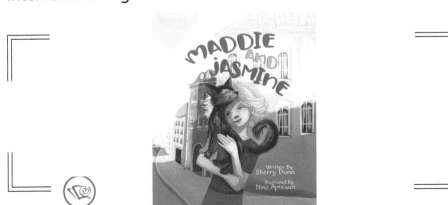

This beautifully written and illustrated book, *Maddie and Jasmine* is not only for kids, but it will also be loved by people of all ages. Anyone who has ever experienced the unconditional love which pets give us will identify with Maddie and will look forward to following her journey with Jasmine in the upcoming series."

— **Andrea Nicholson**, Cat Director,
Dogs & Cats Forever No Kill Shelter

When I first read *Maddie and Jasmine*, I experienced whole body goose-bumps. It is a very special book with an extraordinary message of love. I absolutely love this book. If you know anyone with a child, or you have one, or a grandchild, get a copy of this book for every parent or guardian you know. I believe there is a strong, powerful message contained within.

— **Peggy McColl**, *New York Times*, Best Selling Author

Maddie and Jasmine is an inspiring tale of the deepest love that humans of all ages can relate to! This beautifully written and illustrated story is a perfect gift for a child who may be experiencing bullying, and it is also perfect for children wanting a pet, and for pet rescue advocates. Empowering kids with themes like those found in this book will make a difference in many children's lives!

— **Judy O'Beirn**, International Best Selling Author

MADDIE AND JASMINE

Written By
Sherry Dunn

Illustrated By
Nino Aptsiauri

Published by
Hasmark Publishing
www.hasmarkpublishing.com

Permission should be addressed in writing to Sherry Dunn at sherry@sherrydunn.com

Illustrator: Nino Aptsiauri artninka@gmail.com

Cover Designer: Anne Karklins (anne@hasmarkpublishing.com)

Layout Artist: Amit Dey (amit@hasmarkpublishing.com)

ISBN 13: 978-1-77482-191-6

ISBN 10: 1774821915

Dedication

I dedicate this book to Jasmine, my muse and inspiration for writing *Maddie and Jasmine*. You waited for me at the animal shelter for three years, until I finally found you. You never gave up.

Additionally, I dedicate this book to my previous shelter cats, Marnie, Sally, Remy, Bette, CJ, and Chester, who have gone over the Rainbow Bridge.

Maddie sat outside, alone in her usual place on the playground. Two boys from her class picked the kids they wanted on their soccer teams.

"You," said one of the kids.
He tapped another boy on the arm.

"And I'll pick you for my team," said the other boy, as he touched a tall girl on the shoulder.

Neither of the boys picked Maddie.

No one ever picked Maddie – for anything.

The warm breeze blew Maddie's short, golden, tufted hair in all directions.

"There she is, the dweeb!" someone shouted. "See how crazy she looks with that spiky, golden hair? Like the stray cat that eats out of our trash can."

A stray cat, huh? Thought Maddie. She couldn't wait to get home and talk to Mom.

After school, Maddie raced to her house.
She flung open the front door and shouted,
"Mom, can we get a cat?"

Mom frowned.
"A cat?"

Maddie nodded.

Mom rubbed her chin and seemed to think about it. Finally, she said, "I guess that would be okay."

The next day, a lady named Andrea met Mom and Maddie at the door of the local animal shelter.

"Oh my, look at all the cats," said Mom. "There must be hundreds of them."

Andrea studied Maddie with her tufts of golden hair and unusually colorful outfit. "What type of cat would you like?" she asked her.

Maddie shrugged.

"Well...what about this beautiful cat?"
said Andrea.

Maddie shook her head.

Andrea pointed.
"How about this cute kitten?"

Maddie wrinkled up her nose and shook her head again. Then she noticed a gray cat looking at her and yawning.

"How about that one?" said Andrea.

Maddie frowned and shook her head,
just as an odd-looking little cat with
golden tufts of hair brushed up against her.

"That's Jasmine," said Andrea.

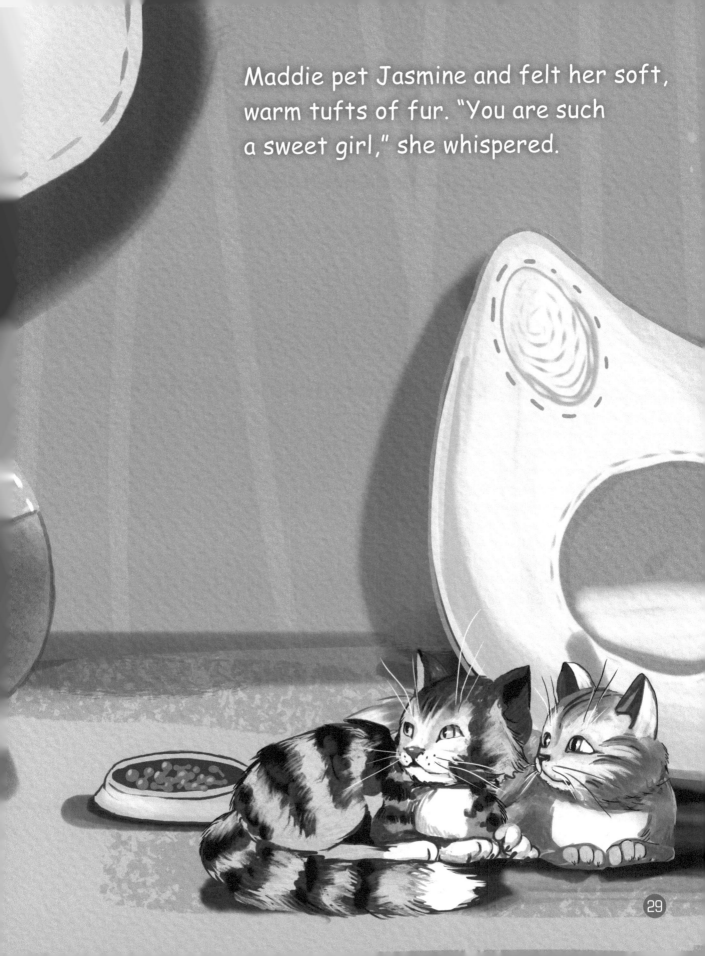

Maddie pet Jasmine and felt her soft, warm tufts of fur. "You are such a sweet girl," she whispered.

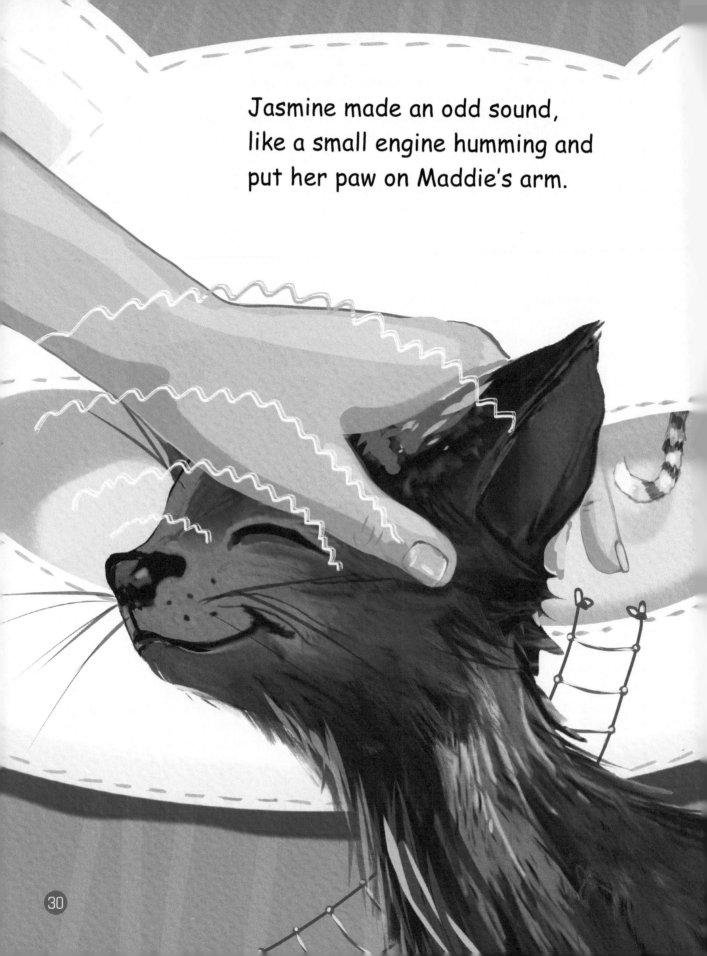

Jasmine made an odd sound, like a small engine humming and put her paw on Maddie's arm.

"Wow," said Andrea.
"I've never heard
Jasmine purr before."

Maddie grinned and announced, "I want Jasmine. She is so sweet and look at her paw, Mom!"

"The paw is pretty cool," said Mom."
It sort of matches your hair. But are
you sure you want to pick this cat?
She's missing some teeth and,
to tell the truth, she looks like a dweeb!"

Yep, a dweeb, thought Maddie. "She's perfect!"

As they were leaving the animal shelter with Jasmine in Maddie's arms, Andrea looked at Maddie and asked, "Out of all the cats here, Maddie, why did you pick Jasmine?"

Jasmine put her golden paw on Maddie's arm again and Maddie smiled. "Oh, I didn't pick Jasmine," she said. "Jasmine picked me!"

The End!

Acknowledgements

The idea for this book came about after I adopted my 7th shelter pet—a bullied and battered little tortoiseshell cat named Jasmine. But my idea didn't really become a children's story until I started working with my friend, writing coach, and fellow children's book author Suzanne Lieurance. I'm tremendously grateful for her guidance and insight that helped me turn a simple narrative about my new pet into a sweet story about bullying, self-acceptance, and the special bond between an awkward girl and a scruffy little cat who rescue each other and become best friends forever.

Writing a children's picture book is harder than I ever imagined. In addition to my writing coach, I would like to thank everyone on the Hasmark Publishing International team who helped me so much through this wonderful journey, giving *Maddie and Jasmine* life. "Thank you to Judy O'Beirn, CEO & President, who said "yes" to publishing Maddie and Jasmine; Jenn Gibson,

Bestseller Campaign Director; Graeme Phillips, Publishing Coordinator; Mary-Kate Luke, Marketing Specialist; Kelly Vurinaris, Media Marketing Consultant; Danielle Martins, Branding Manager; Nino Aptsiauri, Illustrator, who brought Maddie and Jasmine to life with her creativity, sensitivity, and technical artistic proficiency.

A special heartfelt thanks to all the animal shelters I have worked with, each providing and promoting the humane treatment of companion animals under their care. I specifically want to thank Andrea Nicholson for introducing me to little Jasmine at her animal shelter. Thank you to everyone who has adopted shelter pets, including those pets with special needs or are considered seniors.

Lastly, I would like to thank my many, many friends who encouraged me throughout this long journey to publication and who stood by me through all my constant talking about the book and my many drafts.

About the Author

Children's author and animal rescue advocate, Sherry Dunn discovered her passion writing for children after a career in the Human Resources field.

She is an avid reader, and writing seemed to follow naturally.

Sherry is a member of the Society of Children's Book Writers and Illustrators, Children's Book Insider, and the Institute of Children's Literature. She is a contributing editor at Writebythesea.com and a contributing author of *Snap Shots from Real Life, Book 3.* Learn more about Sherry at www.sherrydunn.com.

Sherry lives on Florida's beautiful Treasure Coast with her seventh rescue cat, Jasmine.

When she's not writing, Sherry likes to read, play the piano, work on collage or watercolor art pieces, and work with local art groups and local animal shelters.

For More Information about Sherry, Maddie and Jasmine:

Future books with Hasmark Publishing International:

- Maddie and Jasmine go shopping (book 2)

- Maddie and Jasmine settle in (book 3)

- Lessons from Lucy, a shelter dog

Where to buy the books:

Sold on Amazon, Barnes & Noble, Indiebound

Social media networks/handles:

Facebook: https://www.facebook.com/sherry.dunn.3158/

Instagram: sherrydunnauthor

LinkedIn: https://www.linkedin.com/in/sheryl-dunn-a4234874

BeeKonnected: SherryDunn

Business:

SHERRY DUNN, PawsInPrint, LLC

sherrydunn.com

sherry@sherrydunn.com (business email)

Giving a Voice to Creativity!

From: Circe'
To: Kids who love to write stories!

How would you like to have your story in a book? A real book!
Hearts to be Heard will make that happen.

Get started now at
HeartstobeHeard.com

Also visit HH Kid's Corner for creative writing activities!
HeartstobeHeard.com/kids-corner/

CPSIA information can be obtained
at www.ICGtesting.com
Printed in the USA
LVHW070352180723
752486LV00007B/333